Count on Pablo

by Barbara deRubertis
Illustrated by Rebecca Thornburgh

The Kane Press
New York

Book Design/Art Direction: Roberta Pressel

Library of Congress Cataloging-in-Publication Data

DeRubertis, Barbara.
     Count on pablo/by Barbara deRubertis; illustrated by Rebecca Thornburgh.
        p.   cm.   — (Math matters.   Level 1)
     Summary: Pablo demonstrates how good he is at counting while helping his grandmother, his "abuela," prepare to sell vegetables at the market.
        ISBN: 978-1-57565-090-6 (pbk. : alk. paper)
        [1. Counting—Fiction. 2. Vegetables—Fiction. 3. Markets—Fiction. 4. Grandmothers—
     Fiction. 5. Hispanic Americans—Fiction.]   I. Thornburgh, Rebecca McKillip, ill. II. Title.
     III. Series.
PZ7.D4475Cr 1999
[E]—dc21   98-51119
                                                                                                                        CIP
                                                                                                                        AC

eISBN: 978-1-57565-569-7

20 19

First published in the United States of America in 1999 by Kane Press, Inc.
Printed in China.

MATH MATTERS is a registered trademark of Kane Press, Inc.

Visit us online at **www.kanepress.com**

 Like us on Facebook
facebook.com/kanepress

Follow us on Twitter
@kanepress

It was market day! For the first time, Pablo was going to help his *abuela* (his grandmother) with her market stand. He could hardly wait.

"Is it time to go?" Pablo called.

"Not yet," said Abuela. "We can't go until we pick some things to sell!"

3

"Let's pick FAST," said Pablo.

"Okay, Pablo!" Abuela laughed. "You can pick the limes."

Pablo scurried up the lime tree. "How many should I pick?"

"About twenty," said Abuela. "Nice big ones!"

As Pablo twisted the limes off the tree,
he counted them in a loud voice.

1,   2,   3,   4,   5
6,   7,   8,   9,   10
11, 12, 13, 14, 15
16, 17, 18, 19, 20

"Good counting!" Abuela called.

"Now can we go?" Pablo asked.

"With only limes to sell?" said Abuela. She pointed to a bucket. "First we have to wash these onions and tie them in pairs, like this."

Abuela made a knot with the tops of two onions.

Pablo washed and tied the onions quickly. He got all wet, but he didn't mind.

"Could you count the onions?" Abuela
asked.

"I'll count them by twos. That's a fast way
to count," said Pablo. "Listen, Abuela."
Abuela listened. Pablo counted.

2, 4, 6, 8, 10
12, 14, 16, 18, 20
22, 24, 26, 28, 30
32, 34, 36, 38, 40

"Good counting!" said Abuela.

"Now can we go?" asked Pablo.

"Not yet," said Abuela. "I need you to wash these peppers. Put five in each plastic bag. Then tell me how many peppers we have."

"I'll hurry, Abuela!" said Pablo. He washed the peppers very quickly and got even wetter. But that was okay with Pablo.

"I'll count the peppers by fives," said
Pablo. "That's a faster way to count."

5, 10, 15, 20, 25
30, 35, 40, 45, 50
55, 60, 65, 70, 75
80, 85, 90, 95, 100

"Good counting!" Abuela called.

"Now are we ready?" Pablo asked. Then
he saw that Abuela had five buckets of
tomatoes. "Oh, no!" cried Pablo. "We'll
NEVER get to the market!"

"It's our last job," said Abuela. "We just
have to wash the tomatoes and put ten in
each box."

Before long Pablo had the tomatoes
clean and shiny. But he was a muddy mess!

"I'll count the tomatoes by tens. That's a VERY fast way to count! Listen, Abuela," said Pablo.

10, 20, 30, 40, 50
60, 70, 80, 90, 100
110, 120, 130, 140, 150
160, 170, 180, 190, 200

"Good counting!" said Abuela.

"I almost forgot the cilantro," Abuela said. She tucked a little bunch of the herbs into each box of tomatoes. "Isn't that pretty, Pablo?"

"Very pretty," said Pablo. "But can we PLEASE go to the market now?"

Abuela shook her head. "One more thing needs to be washed!"

Pablo knew she meant HIM. "I'll really hurry!" he said. In no time he was all cleaned up, and they were on their way.

"Finally!" said Pablo.

The market was crowded and noisy. Everywhere Pablo looked, he saw people selling the most wonderful things. There was even a band playing music.

"There are so many stands here today,"
Abuela said.

"I'll make our stand look the best!"
said Pablo.

"Tell me again how many we have of everything," said Abuela. "You count and I'll check."

Abuela's GARDE STAN

So, after Pablo set up the stand, he counted by tens, by fives, by twos, and by ones.

"You are a good helper
and a very good counter,"
said Abuela.

Abuela and Pablo waited for shoppers
to come. Many people were at the market.
But nobody stopped at Abuela's stand.
Nobody at all.

Pablo began to worry. What if Abuela didn't sell anything?

Hours went by. Still they had not sold a thing.

Pablo was getting hungry. "May I buy a bag of tortilla chips from Señor Garcia?" he asked.

"Yes," said Abuela. "I'm a little hungry, too."

Pablo bought a big bag of chips. As he walked back munching, he thought, "I wish I had some . . ." Suddenly he had a great idea. "Abuela!" he shouted.

"What is it?" asked Abuela.

"We could make salsa to go with these chips!"
said Pablo. "Everything we need is right here!
1 lime, 2 onions, 5 peppers, 10 tomatoes . . ."

". . . and a little bunch of cilantro!" said Abuela.

"Making salsa is a wonderful idea!"
Abuela said. "Go buy a pretty bowl
from Señora Martinez. I'll borrow two
knives and a spoon from Señor Garcia."

22

The minute Pablo returned, he began to chop, chop, chop. Bits of tomato and pepper and onion flew everywhere.

"Slow down, Pablo!" said Abuela. "You are chopping too fast!"

Abuela squeezed the lime juice into the bowl. Then Pablo mixed the bright colors together.

"Let's taste it," said Pablo.

Abuela scooped up some salsa with a tortilla chip and popped it in her mouth. "Delicious!" she said.

Pablo tasted the salsa, too. It *was* delicious. "Now we'll see what happens when other people taste our salsa," he said.

Pablo stood right next
to the beautiful bowl of salsa
and the big bag of chips. "Taste
our delicious salsa!" he called.

Soon people were crowding around.
They tasted the salsa. "Delicious!" they said.
"How do you make this salsa?"

Pablo told them. "You need
10 tomatoes, 5 peppers, 2 onions,
1 lime . . ."

". . . and a little bunch of cilantro," said Abuela.

"Then that's what I want!" said a man. "I do, too!" said a dozen voices.

It was very busy. Then it was very quiet. Abeula's stand was empty!

"Abuela," said Pablo, "we sold everything! 20 limes! 40 onions! 100 peppers! 200 tomatoes!"

"And 20 little bunches of cilantro! I've never had such a busy day!" said Abuela.

Abuela's and SALSA GARDEN STAND

Recipe for
PABLO'S
SALSA
Chop and
mix
10 tomatoes
5 peppers
2 onions
Juice of 1 lime
A little bunch
of cilantro

Now on market day, shoppers hurry
to Abuela's stand. There they buy
everything they need to make Pablo's
Salsa. Delicious!

31

Counting Chart

1	2	3	4	5	6	7	8	9	10
11	12	13	14	15	16	17	18	19	20
21	22	23	24	25	26	27	28	29	30
31	32	33	34	35	36	37	38	39	40
41	42	43	44	45	46	47	48	49	50
51	52	53	54	55	56	57	58	59	60
61	62	63	64	65	66	67	68	69	70
71	72	73	74	75	76	77	78	79	80
81	82	83	84	85	86	87	88	89	90
91	92	93	94	95	96	97	98	99	100